Dick and Jane and Vampires

written by Laura Marchesani

Grosset & Dunlap
An Imprint of Penguin Group (USA) Inc.

GROSSET & DUNLAP
Published by the Penguin Group
Penguin Group (USA) Inc., 375 Hudson Street, New York, New York 10014, USA
Penguin Group (Canada), 90 Eglinton Avenue East, Suite 700,
Toronto, Ontario M4P 2Y3, Canada
(a division of Pearson Penguin Canada Inc.)
Penguin Books Ltd., 80 Strand, London WC2R 0RL, England
Penguin Group Ireland, 25 St. Stephen's Green, Dublin 2, Ireland
(a division of Penguin Books Ltd.)
Penguin Group (Australia), 250 Camberwell Road, Camberwell,
Victoria 3124, Australia
(a division of Pearson Australia Group Pty. Ltd.)
Penguin Books India Pvt. Ltd., 11 Community Centre, Panchsheel Park,
New Delhi—110 017, India
Penguin Group (NZ), 67 Apollo Drive, Rosedale, North Shore 0632, New Zealand
(a division of Pearson New Zealand Ltd.)
Penguin Books (South Africa) (Pty.) Ltd., 24 Sturdee Avenue,
Rosebank, Johannesburg 2196, South Africa

Penguin Books Ltd., Registered Offices: 80 Strand, London WC2R 0RL, England

Library of Congress Cataloging-in-Publication data is available.

ISBN 978-0-448-45568-6   10 9 8 7 6 5 4 3 2 1

Contents

We Look and Find

Stories

Come and See

Father said, "Come, Dick.
Come, Jane.
Come and see something."

Father said, "Look, Dick.
Look, Jane.
Look up.
Look up at the sky."

"Is it a bird?" asked Dick.

"No," Jane said.

"It is a bat.
    There is a bat flying
    up in the sky!"

Spot

Come, Dick.

Come and see.

Come and see Spot.

Look, Spot.
Look and see.

Silly Spot.

Do not run.

Funny, funny Spot.

See Jane Go

See Jane.

See Jane go.

See Jane go fast.

Oh, Jane.

Look, look, look.

Oh, Dick.

Funny, funny Dick.

See Puff Play

Come, Dick.

Come and see Puff.

Come and see Puff play.

Look, look.

Puff is not playing.

Puff sees something.

Puff sees something

outside.

Oh, oh, oh.

See Puff jump.

See Puff jump down.

See Puff jump down
and run away.

Run, Puff!

Go, go, go.

Work and Play

See Jane work.
See Jane make
something red.
See Dick work.
See Dick make
something blue.

Oh no!

Look out, Jane!

Look out, Dick!

There is something inside.
There is something inside
the house.

Sally Sees Something

See Sally.

See Sally work.

Oh no!

There is something under
Sally's bed!

Come, Dick.

Come, Jane.

Come and see what is
under Sally's bed.

Oh, Sally.

Funny, funny Sally.

There is nothing there.

There is nothing but
a mess!

Jane Goes Outside

Go, Jane.

Go outside.

Go outside and play.

Oh, oh.

Look, look.

There is something outside.

Run, Jane.
Run away.

Dick Sees Something

Look, Dick.

Look, look.

Look at the red ball.

Look, Jane.

I will get the ball.

I will get the red ball.

Oh, Jane.

Look, look.

That is not the red ball!

Run Away

Run, Dick.
Run, Mother.
Run away!

No, Sally!

Do not go outside.

There is something outside.

Run, Sally, run!
Run away!
Run away and come inside.

We Run and Hide

Stories

Good Night

Good night, Dick.

Good night, Jane.

Good night, Sally.

Sally said, "It is hot.
It is hot inside."
"I can help," Dick said.
"I can help, Sally."

Look out, Jane!

There is something there.

There is something above you.

Go, Go, Go

See Mother go.

Go, go, go.

See Dick go.

See Jane go.

See Sally go.

Look out, Mother!
Look out behind you!

Silly Dick.

Silly Jane.

There is no one there.

Who Is There?

Mother wants something.
The man can help.
That is not a man.
That is something else!

Look, look.

Look, Sally, look.

Look what is there.

Oh, look, Dick and Jane.

Oh, look, Sally.

This is a man.

This is a man who can help.

Look and See

Look, Dick.

Look, Jane.

Look and see.

See Sally.

See, see.

Oh, oh, oh.

Oh, Dick.

Look and see.

Where is Sally?

Look, Jane, look.
Look, Dick, look.
There is Sally.
There is Sally and
something else!

Guess Who?

Come, Dick.

Come, Jane.

Come and see something
funny.

Look, Dick.

Look, Sally.

I see something.

I see something behind us!

Oh, Dick.

Oh, Sally.

What did I see?

Hide and Seek

Look, Spot, look.

Find Dick and Jane.

Go, Spot, go.

Help Sally find Dick.

Help Sally find Jane.

Oh, Spot.

Did you find Dick?

Did you find Jane?

Oh, oh, oh.
It is not Dick.
It is not Jane.
Who is there?

Fun with Father

Look, Jane, look.

There is Father.

Hello, Father.

Oh, oh, oh.

That is not our father.

Run, Jane!
Run, Dick!

Sally, Spot, Tim, and Puff

Look, Spot, look.

See Tim and Puff.

Jump, Spot, jump.

Jump up.

Look and see.

See Sally go.

See Tim go.

See Spot and Puff go.

Oh, oh, oh.

Oh, Sally.

Where is Tim?

Where is Spot?

Where is Puff?

Work, Work, Work

It is time to work.

Work, Dick, work.

Work, Jane, work.

Oh, oh.

There is something here!

Move, move, move.
It is time to work.

We Work and Play

Stories

Dick Climbs Up

Come, Sally.
Come, Jane.
Look up and see.

Look up, Sally.

Look up and see Dick.

See Dick climb up.

See Dick climb up, up, up.

Oh, Jane.

See Dick come down.

See Puff come down.

Down, down, down.

See Vampire go away.

Away, away, away.

Run Away, Vampire

"Here, Dick," said Mother.
"Look what I have.
  A big one for Dick.
  A big one for Jane.
  A little one for Sally."

"Here, Jane. Here, Sally,"
said Dick.
"Put these on.
Put these on and we will
find Vampire."

Look, Vampire, look!
Run, Vampire, run!
Run away fast.

Vampire Helps Jane

Dick said, "Come, Jane.
Come and play ball."
Jane said, "Oh, Dick.
I cannot find the ball.
Come, Dick, come.
Come and find the ball."

Dick said, "I see it.
I see the big ball."
Jane said, "Oh, Dick.
I want the little ball.
Find the little ball."

Dick said, "Look, Jane.
I cannot find the little ball.
Vampire can find the ball.
Vampire can find the little
ball."

Vampire Plays

Oh, Vampire.
See funny Dick.
Dick can play.

Oh, Mother.
Oh, Father.
Jane can play.
Sally can play.

Oh, Father.

See Vampire.

Funny, funny Vampire.

Vampire can play.

Vampire Gets
Dressed

Oh, Jane.

Come and see Mother work.

Mother can make something.

Mother can make something
for Vampire.

Look, Mother, look.

I can work.

I can make something.

I can make something
yellow.

Oh, see funny Vampire.

Funny, funny Vampire.

Dick and Jane Work

Come, Vampire.
Come and see Dick work.
Come and see Jane work.

Look, Vampire, look.

Jane can make something.

Jane can make something pink.

Dick can make something.

Dick can make something blue.

Oh, see funny Jane.
Oh, see funny Dick.
Jane is pink.
Dick is blue.

We Can Help

Dick said, "Look, look.

Here we come.

We can help."

Jane said, "Run, Dick.

Run, run.

We can help."

"Look here," said Sally.
"One is for Dick.
One is for Jane.
One is for Vampire."

"Look, Mother. Look,
Vampire," said Sally.
"Here we come.
Look what we have."

Vampire Jumps
and Plays

Dick said, "Come, Vampire.
Come and jump."
Jane said, "Jump, Vampire.
Jump, Vampire, jump."

Sally said, "Come, Mother.
Come and see Vampire.
Come and see Vampire
jump and play.
Oh, oh.
Vampire is funny."

Mother said, "I can
jump. I can play."
"Oh, oh," said Sally.
"Mother can jump and play.
Oh, oh. Mother is funny.
Let Mother jump, too."

Vampire Plays
House

Come and see the big,
big mother.
See the funny little baby.
Vampire is my baby.
Vampire is my funny little
baby.

I see the big mother.

I see the little baby.

Look, Jane.

See the big father.

Look, Dick, look.

See something funny.

See my baby fly.

See my baby fly away.

Oh, oh, oh.

Sally Dresses Up

Look, Vampire, look.

Oh, oh, oh.
Look at Sally.

Funny, funny Sally.

See What I See

Dick said, "Look, Sally.
Look down here.
See what I see.
See me up here.
See me down here."

"Oh, oh," said Sally.

"I see Tim and me.

I see Puff.

Come, Vampire.

Come and see what I see."

"Oh, oh," said Sally.
"You cannot see.
   You cannot see what I see.
   Do not be sad."

A Friend for
Vampire

Come, Vampire.

Come and see what we have.

Come and see what we have for you.

Look, Vampire, look.

Look and see.

Look at our new friend!

Happy, happy Vampire!

A Happy Ending

Dick is happy.

Jane is happy.

Sally is happy.

Vampire is happy.
Happy, happy, happy!

We are happy with our
friends!